THE NIGHT KNIGHTS

WORDS BY GIDEON STERER
PICTURES BY CORY GODBEY

ABRAMS BOOKS FOR YOUNG READERS, NEW YORK

When the sun fades . . .
and we fall asleep,

some believe it to be a time of monsters.

Indeed, some are sure of it.

But if this is true, is it not strange that not once,

not once,

has a child ever been

TAKEN,

or # GOTTEN,

or # BIT?

Is it not strange that not once,

not once,

has a # MONSTER

ever *actually* been seen?

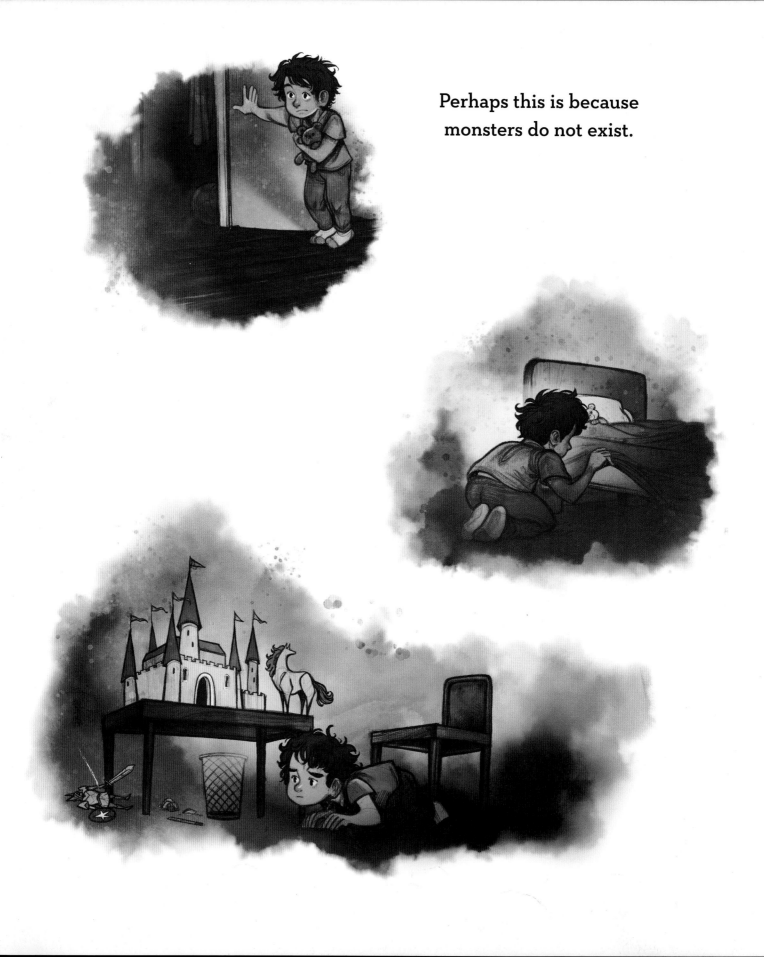

Perhaps this is because
monsters do not exist.

Or, perhaps, as some believe,
it is because *night brings something else . . .*
something armored,
something ancient,
something that defends us through the dark.

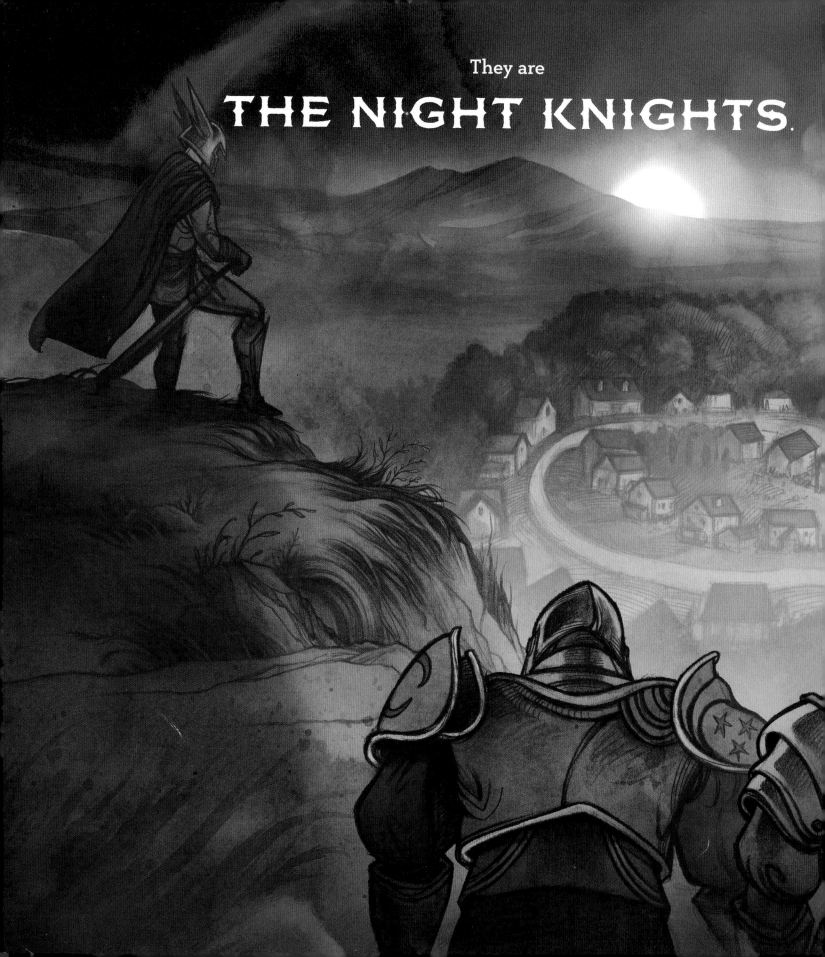

They are

THE NIGHT KNIGHTS.

And as the world turns
off its lights . . .

they take their place.

With broad shield
and heavy sword,

at our doors stand the Guardians of Gates.

Tonight, nothing passes.
Tonight, nothing knocks.

Above us, flying flags of sleep,

the Watchmen
do not blink.

Tonight, nothing scampers.
Tonight, nothing sneaks.

Beyond us,

through fields,
through streets,

the Horsemen charge,
the Horsemen hunt.

Tonight, they ride,
and nothing hides,

for all will be outrun.

Clothed in cloaks,
they draw their bows.

The Archers aim.
The Archers wait.

Their arrows fill the sky like stars,
and burn against the black.

Toward us flies
the Midnight Flock . . .

for the Keeper of Owls
has called.

And as they search
from skies above . . .

a fleet patrols the sea.

Soon, if you wish them,

arrive the Knights of Near.

Smaller, but of equal strength . . .

they stand where there is fear.

But perhaps you will *still* be afraid.

Perhaps when dark is darkest,

you will hear

a **BUMP**,

or **THUMP**,

or **SCRATCH**.

Perhaps then you will know
that a monster is close.

You will *know* . . .

that a **MONSTER**

is coming.

But if this happens,
wait just a moment,

then another,

and you will see that over
and over,

again and again . . .

nothing ever comes.

Perhaps there is no such thing as monsters.

But even if there is, it wouldn't matter . . .

for this room is your castle,

this house is your kingdom,

and tonight,

as you sleep,

as you dream . . .

an army stands for you.

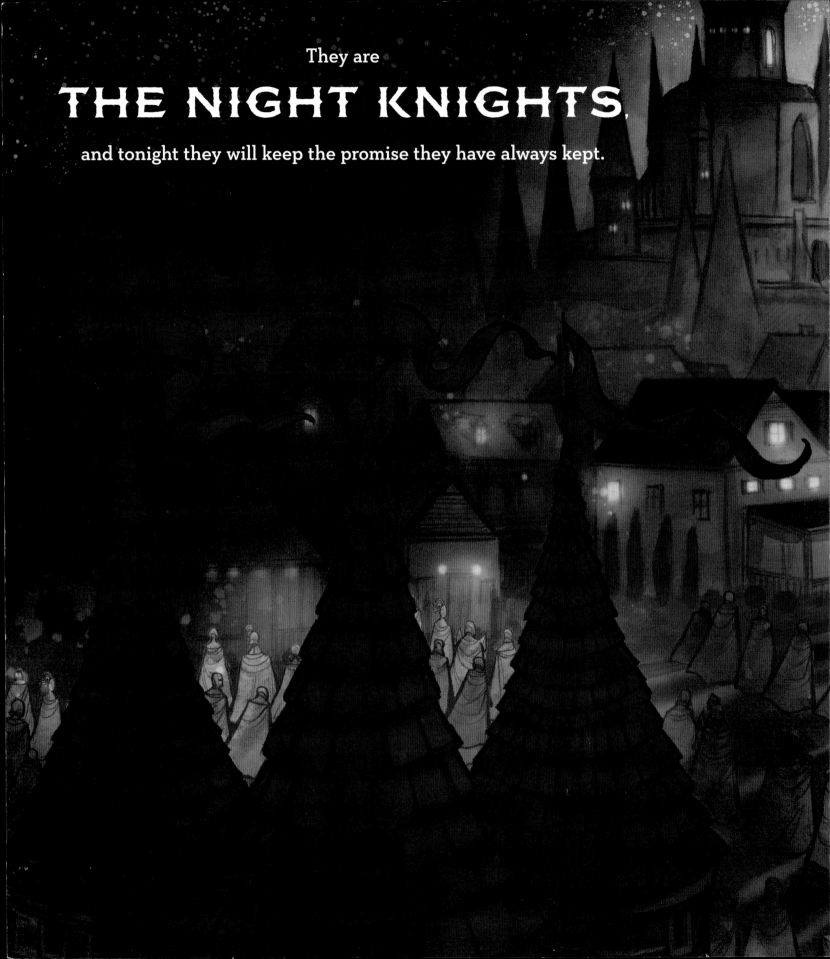

They are

THE NIGHT KNIGHTS,

and tonight they will keep the promise they have always kept.

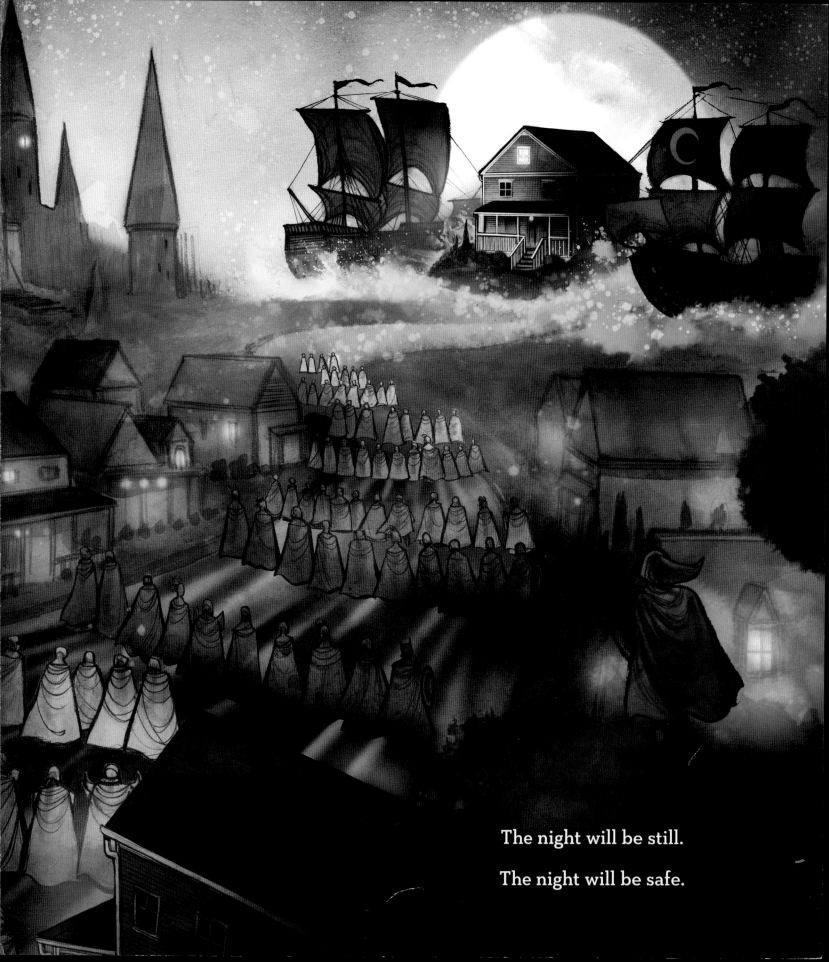

The night will be still.

The night will be safe.

Cataloging-in-Publication Data has been applied for
and may be obtained from the Library of Congress.
ISBN 978-1-4197-2846-4

Text copyright © 2018 Gideon Sterer
Illustrations copyright © 2018 Cory Godbey
Book design by Chad W. Beckerman

ABRAMS The Art of Books
195 Broadway, New York, NY 10007
abramsbooks.com